Saralee loves Rosh Hashanah, the Jewish New Year. And why not? Rosh Hashanah is a joyous holiday that celebrates the birthday of the world. It's a time to reflect, sing, pray, gather with loved ones, and, of course, eat . . . which is the part Saralee, a budding baker, loves most. Apple cake is a classic Rosh Hashanah treat, as is any apple dessert, but perhaps the most traditional dish at the Jewish New Year is simply apple slices dipped in honey, which signify that the coming year should be sweet. "A sweet new year, / a sweet new year, / make a wish for a sweet new year," sings Zadie, and that's what the characters in this story do: They make wishes for a year that is as sweet as a honey-dipped apple.

The characters in this book also make a few mistakes. The High Holidays of Rosh Hashanah and Yom Kippur, the Day of Atonement, are a time for us to think about mistakes we've made in the past year and consider how we can improve in the next one. The New Year is a time to practice *teshuvah*, Hebrew for "returning." The most important Rosh Hashanah wish is to become better versions of ourselves. That helps make for the sweetest New Year of all.

A Note from PJ Library®

Think about the challenges Saralee faces as she tries to figure out Zadie's recipe and protect her family's business, and ask yourself some questions:

- What assumptions does Saralee make about Harold Horowitz? Are they correct?

- When Saralee first meets Harold, she decides that sharing one of his cookies "would be a betrayal." Do you agree?

- At the end of the story, Saralee accepts one of Harold's cookies. Do you think they'll become friends? Why?

You can make an apple cake like the one Saralee makes. Try the recipe on the inside back cover of this book, or visit pjlibrary.org/applecake for a few more dessert ideas. No matter which recipe you choose, take a cue from Zadie and make a wish for the coming year.

About PJ Library

The gift of PJ Library, a family engagement program, is made possible by many generous supporters, your local Jewish community, and the Harold Grinspoon Foundation. PJ Library shares Jewish culture and values through quality children's books that reflect the diversity of Jewish customs and practice. To learn more about the program and ways to connect to activities in your area, visit pjlibrary.org.

Once Upon an Apple Cake
A Rosh Hashanah Story

By Elana Rubinstein

Illustrated by Jennifer Naalchigar

For Mom and Dad. I love you!
— E. R.

For Will and Phoebe
— J. N.

Apples & Honey Press
An imprint of Behrman House
Millburn, New Jersey 07041
www.applesandhoneypress.com

Text copyright © 2019 by Elana Rubinstein
Illustrations copyright © 2019 by Behrman House

ISBN 978-1-68115-549-4

Library of Congress Cataloging-in-Publication Data

Names: Rubinstein, Elana, author. | Naalchigar, Jennifer, illustrator.
Title: Once upon an apple cake : a Rosh Hashanah story / by Elana Rubinstein
; illustrated by Jennifer Naalchigar.
Description: Millburn, New Jersey : Apples & Honey Press, an imprint of
Behrman House, [2019] | Summary: Ten-year-old Saralee Siegal, who loves to
cook and help at her family's restaurant, has a heightened sense of smell
but still cannot identify what makes her Zadie's special cake the best.
Identifiers: LCCN 2018050066 | ISBN 9781681155494
Subjects: | CYAC: Smell--Fiction. | Baking--Fiction. | Grandfathers--Fiction.
| Restaurants--Fiction. | Rosh ha-Shanah--Fiction. | Jews--United
States--Fiction.
Classification: LCC PZ7.1.R8276 Onc 2019 | DDC [Fic]--dc23 LC record
available at https://lccn.loc.gov/2018050066

Design by NeuStudio
Edited by Dena Neusner
Printed in the United States of America

1 3 5 7 9 8 6 4 2

081929.1K1/B1446/A8

Contents

Chapter One
My Super-Nose

Zadic says I have a secret weapon. Only it's not a *normal* secret weapon, like super strength or invisibility.

The truth is, I have a super-nose.

Yep—a super-nose.

Now, let's be clear about something. I don't use my nose to sword fight, lift weights, or climb walls. I can't sneeze out fairy dust, and I certainly don't have rainbow boogers.

Most people think my nose is perfectly

normal, thank you very much. Even Aunt Lotte says it's "as cute as a button."

But trust me, my nose is a force to be reckoned with.

Take last Sunday, for example. Zadie and I were busy in the restaurant kitchen. Saucepans simmered on the stove. Bread baked in the oven.

"Saralee," Zadie called, "take a sniff of my wonderful *zoop*!"

Zadie has gray hair flecked with white. He likes to say *zoop* instead of *soup*. I think it's a weird grandpa thing.

I set down my mixing spoon and hovered over the soup pot. The steam swirled around me and I breathed in deep.

"Hmmm," I said. "I smell . . ."

I stopped and narrowed my eyes at Zadie. He crossed his arms and narrowed his eyes at me. Then I let loose.

"Nine carrots, two celery sticks, four sweet potatoes, three onions, chicken stock, two tablespoons of dill, one parsnip, twenty matzah balls, a dash of salt, and a wee, tiny, itty-bitty pinch of pepper."

See, this is what I'm talking about. I can smell things like no one's business.

After smelling the soup again himself, Zadie pinched my cheeks.

"My Saralee Siegel . . . ," he muttered. "With a nose like that, you'll rule the world."

I love my zadie. He's the head chef of Siegel House, our family restaurant. He smells like peppermint and just the slightest bit of corned beef on rye.

Even though I'm only ten, I'm Zadie's executive assistant. Mostly I do cool stuff, like brew pickle brine, flip pancakes, and add spices to spaghetti sauce. But sometimes I have to do some uncool stuff, like sniff out all the rotten food in the back of the refrigerator.

Anyway, Zadie and I spent all Sunday afternoon in the restaurant kitchen. We made baked chicken and roasted potatoes. We made hundreds of sandwiches. We cooked and cooked and cooked until all the customers left for the night.

When the moon appeared in the sky, Zadie stopped cooking. He washed the dishes and then grinned at me.

"Oh, Saralee," he said, "it's time. . . ."

At first I didn't know what he was talking about. But then I saw his smile. Zadie gets a smile like that only once a year.

"Oh no . . . ," I said.

He grinned even wider. "Oh yes. Prepare to be bested by your old grandpa."

See, my nose is an incredible thing. I can pretty much smell any food in the world and tell you exactly what's in it. But there's one dish I just can't seem to get right. I try every year. And every year I fail.

"It's time to make apple cake for Rosh Hashanah!" sang Zadie.

He had a smug look on his face.

Rosh Hashanah is the Jewish New Year. It's a very important holiday here at Siegel House Restaurant. We decorate the tables with honey jars (to wish our customers a sweet new year) and give out candy bags.

For Rosh Hashanah, we rewrite the menus, clean out the cookie display, and iron our aprons. We try to make everything just a tad bit nicer than the year before.

But the absolute best part of Rosh Hashanah is my zadie's apple cake. It's actually famous. People travel far and wide to get their hands on a slice. Last year, the line curved all the way to town hall.

Every year, Zadie puts a blindfold over my eyes and whips up his famous apple cake batter. Then, when everything is all mixed together, he tells me to list all of the ingredients.

When I cover my eyes and plug up my ears, my sense of smell gets unbelievably strong. I call this going into over-smell.

But no matter how powerful my nose becomes, the same thing always happens. I can smell the flour, oil, sugar, eggs, salt, honey, baking soda, vanilla, cinnamon, and two thinly sliced apples. But there is one last ingredient I can't figure out.

It's so infuriating! The mystery ingredient smells sweet yet spicy, zesty yet bland, tart yet un-tart.

It makes absolutely no sense. And it's my life's mission to figure it out.

I looked at Zadie. He was taking out his baking pans.

"I'm going to get it right this year," I called to him.

Zadie handed me a blindfold and then winked. "We'll see. . . ."

Chapter Two
Pantry Disaster

"You know," Zadie said, laughing, "this year's gonna be a bit different. Perfection on a Platter is making Rosh Hashanah apple cake too."

Perfection on a Platter is the new restaurant in town. Last week was the grand opening.

"Ha," I mumbled. "I bet those copycats will get laughed out of town."

Zadie gave me a look.

"Oh, don't worry so much," he said. "Everyone round here has a big appetite. There's more than enough room for two restaurants."

But I shook my head.

Zadie is always *way* too nice. Once he gave out free pickles to everyone in town. We ran out of sour dills before lunchtime.

Plus, didn't Zadie know that this new restaurant was trouble?

They were *already* trying to compete with our apple cake. That couldn't be a good sign. Obviously those silly fools had no idea who they were dealing with. No one, and I mean no one, can re-create my zadie's apple cake recipe.

"All righty then," said Zadie, "get that blindfold on lickety-split. And don't you peek. I just need to grab my ingredients from the downstairs pantry."

I tied the blindfold over my eyes. I could hear Zadie thumping down the steps. He was singing a Rosh Hashanah song.

A sweet new year.
A sweet new year.
Make a wish for a sweet new year.

As I sat there in the dark, I touched my nose with my pointer finger.

"Come on, nose," I whispered out loud. "You can do this."

I was feeling pretty confident. I mean, last year I was only nine. My nose receptacles hadn't fully developed yet. But this year—

THWACK, CLUNK, CLANG, THUD!

Then silence.

"Zadie?" I called. "Zadie? Are you okay?"

My voice came out all squeaky.

"Zadie?" I called again.

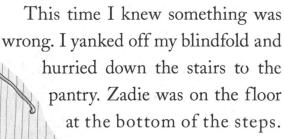

This time I knew something was wrong. I yanked off my blindfold and hurried down the stairs to the pantry. Zadie was on the floor at the bottom of the steps. His eyes were closed, and he was holding his leg really tightly.

"Saralee," he whispered. "I hit my head . . . and I think I broke my leg. OW!"

There was a big red blotch on his bald spot. Zadie let go of his leg and touched it.

"*Oy vey*," he groaned.

Without thinking twice, I ran into the dining room. My aunts and uncle were closing down the restaurant. Uncle Sam was fishing the extra pickles out of the pickle bar. There was pickle juice all down his apron, and he had accidentally squashed a sour dill under his foot. A few feet away, Aunt Bean was cleaning the glass dessert case with a toothbrush. And as usual, Aunt Lotte was doing everyone the favor of "just watching."

"Snickerdoodle!" I called.

They all looked up. In our family, *snickerdoodle* is the secret code word for emergency. We use a code word because we don't want to upset any customers who might be around.

Only a few seconds later, everyone was crowded around Zadie in the pantry.

"Oh dear," muttered Aunt Bean. She started wiping Zadie's head with a wet wipe.

Uncle Sam tried to get some ice from the freezer, but he tripped over a pile of canned beans. The cans scattered everywhere.

Aunt Lotte popped her bubble gum. "I'll call an ambulance," she muttered.

Even my grandmother, who I call Bubbie, was concerned.

"An ambulance?" she asked. "Where?"

Bubbie is always a bit confused about things. She wears nightgowns like fancy dresses. She also likes to make jewelry out of dried noodles.

We all gathered around Zadie and waited for the ambulance. Zadie held onto my hand.

"Saralee," he said, "there's something you should . . ."

But Aunt Bean interrupted him. "Oh, shush," she said. "Don't try and talk now. This is not the time to exert yourself."

"But I need to . . . ," Zadie tried again.

This time he was interrupted by a loud whirring sound. It was the ambulance. Only a moment later, a man and a woman in hospital uniforms ran down the stairs to the pantry.

I started to panic when they lifted Zadie onto a stretcher. The two of us were like peanut butter and jelly, french fries and ketchup, beef and barley.

He couldn't go!

Not now, not ever.

Chapter Three
Poof!

The man and the woman carried Zadie up the stairs and out the front door. They lifted him into the ambulance.

"WAIT!" Zadie shouted.

Everything stopped. The spot on his head had swelled up into a little bump. It was the color of a perfectly ripe raspberry.

"Oh, goodness gracious," Zadie cried. "There's so much to do. The restaurant! The apple cakes!"

Zadie pointed to my aunts and uncle. "Promise me you'll run things smoothly while I'm gone. Do *not* have any snickerdoodle moments, please."

Aunt Bean's eyes grew wide. "We promise. Siegel House will be in tip-top shape when you get back. I'll make everything sparkly clean."

Then Zadie beckoned me closer. "Saralee, you're my one and only executive assistant. Your aunts and uncle need to focus on the restaurant. But you, my dear, are in charge of the apple cakes. Rosh Hashanah is only five days away. Make our customers slappy . . ."

"Slappy?" I asked, my voice trembling.

Zadie shook his head. "No I mean *tappy* . . . no *flappy* . . . Wait, what's the word?"

I looked up at my family in horror.

"Do you mean . . . *happy*?" I asked. "Make our customers *happy*?"

Zadie smacked his forehead. "Yes, *happy*! That's what I meant."

Really, I don't cry a lot. But at that moment, I

felt this lump forming in the back of my throat. Something was wrong with Zadie. He never *ever* gets his words mixed up.

"But I can't make the apple cakes," I whispered. "I don't know the secret ingredient."

Zadie touched his raspberry bump and squished his eyebrows together.

"Secret ingredient?" he asked.

I nodded. "Just tell me. I'll make those apple cakes quick as a bunny."

Zadie opened his mouth to speak, but nothing came out.

"Come on, Zadie," I pressed. "You've gotta spill the beans."

This time Zadie frowned.

"Are you sure there was a secret ingredient?" he asked.

I couldn't believe what I was hearing!

"Yes, Zadie," I blurted. "You know, sweet yet spicy, zesty yet bland, tart yet un-tart?"

Zadie shut his eyes real tight for a few moments.

"I can't . . . I can't seem to remember it," Zadie said. "It's like the memory is gone, *poof.* I'm sorry, Saralee."

I must've looked completely heartbroken, because Zadie pinched my nose between his fingers.

"Now don't you worry," he said softly. "Your super-nose will figure it out. I believe in you. We *all* believe in you."

"Wa— wait . . . ," I stuttered.

But Zadie wrinkled his nose in pain and then kind of groaned. The hospital woman quickly closed the big white doors.

"What's wrong with him?" I asked her.

She climbed into the front seat.

"With a fall like that," she said, "your grandfather's memory might be a bit fuzzy for a while. We've got to get him to the hospital now."

I watched as the ambulance sped down the street and disappeared around the corner.

I sniffed.

I could smell the grass wet with dew.

I could smell the tiniest bit of salt on the wind.

I thought about Perfection on a Platter and a long line outside their door instead of ours. I thought about Zadie's fuzzy memory and the raspberry bump on top of his head.

How could this happen? I thought. *And how can I make those apple cakes?*

Chapter Four
Order Forms

The next morning, everything was chaos without Zadie. Uncle Sam tried making twenty breakfast sandwiches at once. Aunt Bean trailed behind with a bottle of cleaning spray. Siegel House would officially open in two minutes, and the kitchen looked like one big disaster zone.

"Hey, Saralee," called Uncle Sam, "can you pass me a—"

CRASH!

A platter of scrambled eggs tumbled to the floor. Aunt Bean dove out of the way, holding her cleaning spray like a shield.

I didn't have time to help, though. Finding the secret ingredient was first on my list today. I was about to close my eyes and go into over-smell when I felt a poke in my back.

I whirled around.

"Wanna play?" asked my little cousin, Josh. "Can I do an *eezamination?*"

Josh was still wearing his skeleton pajamas. He thrust his toy doctor's bag in my face.

"Not now, Josh," I grumbled.

"Please, please, *pulllleeeeeeeeeeeeeeeeze?*" he asked.

I love my little cousin. But he's only five, and sometimes he's really annoying. He thinks he's a doctor and is always trying to shove his plastic thermometer in my ear.

"C'mon," begged Josh. "Lemme take your blood present."

"Don't you mean blood pressure?" I asked him.

He nodded. "Uh-huh. Blood present."

I didn't have time for these shenanigans. Zadie had given me an important mission. I was his executive assistant, and I couldn't let him down. So I zipped my lips and took a deep sniff.

The smells at Siegel House Restaurant this morning were strong. I could smell fluffy eggs with salt and pepper. I could smell buttery scones filled with blueberry jam. And then there were waffles—extra crispy and covered in syrup. I closed my eyes and tried to think of every ingredient in the room.

I was on item number 1,008 when Josh pinched my elbow.

"Saralee," he said, "you're doing that smelling thingy again."

I opened my eyes. Josh had taken out his toy

Sweet juicy melon
ground coffee beans
crunchy granola
sweet cream
ricotta cheese
pineapple juice
whipped butter
raspberry compote
tea leaves
cinnamon
rosemary
parsley
avocado
oregano
oatmeal
olive oil

stethoscope and was pressing
it to my back. I was so busy smelling things,
I hadn't even noticed.

I looked at the clock again. It was time for
the restaurant to open!

Josh and I scampered into the dining room
just in time to see tiny Aunt Bean change her
germ-protectant gloves and open the door. Customers rushed inside.

"Hey, Saralee," called Mr. Rosen.

Mr. Rosen is the principal of my elementary school. He eats at Siegel House almost every morning. As usual, Mr. Rosen had on a brown suit with a brown tie. He opened up his brown briefcase and took out a slip of paper.

"Don't lose this," he said, giving it to me.

I looked down and immediately felt butterflies in my stomach.

"It's my order form," Mr. Rosen explained. "You know, for the Rosh Hashanah apple cake."

I gulped.

"And speaking of apple cake—how is your zadie doing? Feeling okay after his fall last night?"

That's the thing about living in a small town. News travels fast.

"He's fine," I squeaked. "Hopefully he'll be home in a few days."

Mr. Rosen sighed. "What a shame. Well, if you guys aren't making apple cakes this year, I can always get mine from Perfection on a Platter."

Chapter Five
All Muddled Up

Ny face turned red.

Perfection on a Platter? No . . .

I tried to fake a smile, but my lips wobbled.

"Oh," I said, "I . . . it's fine. We are definitely making apple cakes this year. Don't you worry."

I couldn't let our customers order their apple cakes from that copycat restaurant! Rosh Hashanah was only four days away. It was time to get busy.

Soon, tons of customers were handing me

their order forms. By the time I got home from school that afternoon, Aunt Bean was alphabetizing a tall stack of order forms in the kitchen.

"Sheesh," she muttered to herself. "So much work, work, work."

I bit my fingernail.

That was a *huge* pile of order forms.

The rest of my family sat around the kitchen island eating leftovers. It was that strange time between lunch and dinner. The tables were empty, and everything was oddly quiet.

Everyone looked absolutely exhausted.

Uncle Sam had taken over the cooking. He was wearing Zadie's chef's hat, but it was way

too small for him. It looked like a white mushroom on his head.

Even Aunt Lotte "helped." Aunt Lotte is the official Siegel House waitress. She usually spends her days shouting orders into the kitchen, real loud. But today she had to wash dishes too. Boy, did she grumble and groan. After her third dish, I'm pretty sure she just ran her hands under the water instead of scrubbing.

Uncle Sam helped himself to his third sandwich.

"So, Saralee," he started, "have you figured out the secret . . . ?"

But he didn't finish his sentence.

RING RING, went the phone.

Aunt Bean wiped down the receiver before answering it.

"Siegel House Restaurant," she said sweetly. "Yes . . . uh-huh . . . oh dear . . ."

We all got quiet.

"It's the hospital," Aunt Bean mouthed to us.

"My, my . . ." Aunt Bean breathed into the phone. "All righty . . . Well, not me. Hospitals are too germy. But, yes, someone will be there."

She hung up with a *click*.

"Well?" asked Uncle Sam.

"Poor Zadie," Aunt Bean said. "He's having a hard time. He's all confused and doesn't remember falling yesterday. Now he thinks our customers are going hungry. The doctor says he has temporary amnesia."

"Temporary amnesia?" I asked. "What's that?"

Aunt Bean squeezed some hand sanitizer onto her palm. She rubbed it around and around, looking worried.

"It's when your memory gets all muddled and shook up," she said. "It will go away eventually. But it does take some time."

Uncle Sam shoved the rest of his sandwich into his mouth.

"I'll go to the hospital," he said. "He needs to know Siegel House is fine and dandy. The rest of you, remember what Zadie said last night. No snickerdoodle moments. Let's make him proud."

"I'll come too," I chimed in.

Maybe I could help remind him about the whole apple cake fiasco?

"You can't go, Saralee," said Aunt Bean.

"What! Why?" I asked.

Aunt Bean brushed some crumbs off the counter. "Do you know how many germs you have on those fingers? No kids. They just said so on the phone."

I couldn't believe it! I wasn't just an ordinary kid. I was Zadie's executive assistant. And plus, I had a mystery to solve. Didn't that count for anything?

Uncle Sam scrambled around for his keys.

"Hey, don't forget to ask about the secret ingredient," I called as he ran out the door.

When the car rumbled down the driveway, I felt my eyes fill with tears. This just wasn't fair. My whole body felt heavy, like a giant sack of russet potatoes.

"What's wrong, Pookie Wookie?" asked Bubbie.

Bubbie calls everyone Pookie Wookie. It's because she can't remember anyone's name.

"What if I can't find the secret ingredient?" I asked her. "What if I never *ever* figure it out? I just wish I had the answer already."

Bubbie tucked a strand of hair behind my ear. Then she took a twisty noodle necklace out of her pocket and slipped it over my head.

"Sweet Pookie Wookie," she cooed, touching the little macaronis with her wrinkled hand. "Never say never. A little wish goes a long way."

Chapter Six
The Strangers

When Uncle Sam came back from the hospital, he stubbed his toe on the front door.

"Ouch," he hollered, jumping up and down.

Josh rushed forward with a magnifying glass.

"Lemme see the boo-boo," he called.

But I waved Josh away.

"Did you get the secret ingredient?" I asked Uncle Sam.

He shook his head. "Oh boy, Zadie's noggin is all confused. He thought we ran out of breadsticks, even though he made loads of them yesterday. But the doctor says this happens with old folks sometimes. He'll get his memories back, don't you worry."

I looked down at my shoes. Today was not going as I had planned. What if Zadie didn't get his memories back before Rosh Hashanah?

I felt sick even just thinking about it.

Around five o'clock, the Early Bird Club came for dinner. The Early Birds wear binoculars around their necks and practice bird calls over spaghetti and meatballs. This evening they were louder than normal. They filled the dining room with chirping and tweeting.

As I served the breadsticks, I heard the front door open.

I looked up.

A group of guests I'd never seen before streamed inside. They wore crisp suits the color of chocolate pudding.

"Well, hello, Pookie Wookies," called Bubbie.

"Welcome, welcome. I have a special table just for you."

Bubbie led the guests to a table in the back.

Aunt Lotte poked me in the arm.

"Oh boy," she whispered. "They look like a bunch of sour dills. I'm not dealing with that today."

She handed me the menus. "Go see what they want."

I headed toward their table. The guests reeked of sugar. They overwhelmed my nose with cotton candy, and caramel, and sugary icing. But underneath all that was the smell of old, stale grease, like when you use that fryer one too many times.

Before I could say a word, one of the guests rapped her bony knuckles on the table. She had a pinched face, and her hair was pulled back into a bun.

"We'll start with iced coffee with extra ice and extra sugar," she barked. "Make it cold."

I gulped. Zadie always says to be polite even when people don't deserve it.

"Coming right up," I said.

I gave them my best smile and ran back to the kitchen. I poured the coffee and was putting the glasses on a tray for Aunt Lotte when I heard a rustling sound.

"What was that?" I asked Uncle Sam.

He looked up from his snack. He still had a donut crammed into his cheek.

I heard the rustling sound again.

That's when I saw something strange. Peeking out from behind the kitchen island was a . . . a leg.

It was a kid-sized leg. I sniffed and smelled that sweet, sugary smell again. That wasn't Josh's leg. So whose was it?

I quickly grabbed a mixing spoon and ran toward the island. I rounded the corner and couldn't believe my eyes.

There, scavenging through the island's bottom drawer, was a kid I'd never seen before.

"Stop right there!" I called.

The kid wore a button-down shirt and a green tie. His hands were full of top secret Siegel House recipes. We keep them in the bottom island drawer so they won't get messy while we cook.

When he saw me, the kid quickly let go of the recipes and slammed the drawer shut. Then he started scratching his bright red hair. His locks were gelled into a spike near his forehead.

"What do you think you're doing back here?" I asked. "The kitchen is for family members only."

Suddenly I noticed that there were letters stitched into his tie. In fancy, curly script it said *POP.*

POP?

What was POP?

Then everything clicked. Perfection on a Platter! This kid was spying on us. He was looking through our recipes, for goodness' sake! And those suited strangers weren't customers, they were the enemy.

I knew it! Perfection on a Platter was up to no good.

Chapter Seven
The Showdown

"**S**nickerdoodle!" I called.

This was a *major* emergency moment.

Before I could catch him, the kid darted out of the kitchen and into the dining room.

I ran after him.

"It's them!" I shouted. I pointed to the table full of suited men and a woman. "It's Perfection on a Platter! They're spying on us."

The Early Bird Club stopped twittering. They all pulled out their binoculars and ogled.

My entire family gathered around me. Josh whipped out a plastic mallet from his doctor's bag. He held it like a sword.

The red-haired kid was hiding behind the pickle bar now. All that was showing was his pointy hair spike.

The Perfection on a Platter family got to their feet.

The bony woman stepped forward.

"Your days of feeding this town are over," she said. "We are going to make the best, most delicious apple cakes this Rosh Hashanah. You can kiss your teeny tiny restaurant good-bye."

I could smell her greasy breath from across the room.

Aunt Lotte put her hands on her hips.

"Oh yeah?" she said. "Then why are you spying on us? Couldn't think of your own recipes?"

"Oh, you're going down big-time," said a suited man. "We're going to whip you like cream."

Soon everyone was throwing insults like there was no tomorrow.

"Ha!" someone said. "You'll be nothing but mashed potatoes when we're done with you."

"Your cooking is so bad, I can't tell the difference between your meatloaf and your brownies."

"Well, your cookies are like hockey pucks."

"No, *your* cookies are like hockey pucks."

"No, *your* . . ."

One of the suited men put his grimy hands on the glass cookie case.

Aunt Bean's eyes grew wide.

"Get your dirty hands off my case," she said in a squeaky voice.

The Perfection on a Platter family snickered.

"This won't be the last you see of us," said the bony woman.

She pulled the redheaded kid out from behind the pickle bar.

"Come dear," she said, leading the family out the door, as the Early Bird Club started twittering again.

Even though Perfection on a Platter was gone, my whole family was on edge for the rest of the night. Aunt Bean was so nervous, she rearranged the menus sixteen different times.

When we closed the restaurant for the night, everyone trudged up the stairs in a bad mood. Well, everyone except for me.

I stared around at the dark, empty kitchen. This was truly turning into a catastrophe.

I love my zadie, but he was wrong about Perfection on a Platter. They were truly awful. Obviously, there was only room for one restaurant in this town.

I bit my lip. How in the world was I going to figure out the secret ingredient?

My nose was failing me.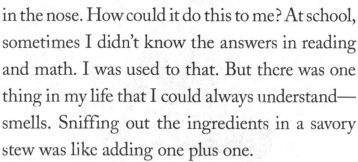

I felt like I wanted to punch my nose right in the nose. How could it do this to me? At school, sometimes I didn't know the answers in reading and math. I was used to that. But there was one thing in my life that I could always understand—smells. Sniffing out the ingredients in a savory stew was like adding one plus one.

I thought about Zadie all alone in his hospital bed so far away. I had to make this apple cake. Zadie was counting on me. The family was counting on me. In fact, the whole town was counting on me. If I didn't make these apple cakes soon, people would start ordering from Perfection on a Platter.

Tomorrow was Tuesday. That meant Rosh Hashanah was only three days away. I needed to act fast.

"Come on, nose," I whispered into the darkness, "be my secret weapon."

Chapter Eight
Harold the Horror

School the next day was an absolute disaster. The second I sat down at my desk, I knew something stinky was in the air. It was that terrible smell again: overly sweet with a hint of grease.

"Class," said my teacher, Mrs. Stearns, "I am so excited to introduce a new member of our community."

It couldn't be, I thought. *It really, really, really couldn't be.*

But unfortunately, it was.

The redheaded Perfection on a Platter boy walked to the front of the class. He looked down at his shoes and played with his tie. Speaking of which, a TIE? Who wears a tie to school?

Mrs. Stearns smiled. "This is Harold Horowitz. As you've probably heard, Harold and his family just moved here. They opened that delicious Perfection on a Platter restaurant uptown."

The stink in my nose grew even stinkier.

"Humph," I mumbled under my breath. "His name should be Harold the Horror."

During lunch, I opened my lunch box and took out my super-sour dill pickle, my corned-beef-on-rye sandwich (extra mustard), and my black and white cookie. Usually, all the other kids ask for a bite of my sandwich or a nibble of my cookie.

But today, they all hovered around Harold.

I narrowed my eyes as he unzipped his lunch box. He took out a bag of cookies. I could smell the sugar from across the table. The cookies were drippy, and gooey, and covered with icing.

"Wow," said my friend Rachel Rubin. "Where did you get those cookies?"

"I made them," said Harold.

When he spoke, I saw that he had a mouth full of braces.

Harold got up from the lunch table and started passing out the cookies to everyone in our class.

"We're not supposed to share food," I said.

But no one was listening. All my friends were too busy *oohing* and *aahing* over those cookies.

Finally, Harold the Horror came over to me.

"Saralee Siegel, right?" he asked.

I nodded. I tried to think of an insult, but I just couldn't. I was too busy looking at the cookies. They weren't *actually* as drippy or gooey as I had thought. They were just sugar cookies.

He held one out to me. "Want one?"

The truth was that I *did* want one. I mean, they didn't smell like my Aunt Bean's heavenly Sugar Cookie Supremes. But the decoration was . . . it was truly a work of art. Harold had decorated the cookies with tiny flowers and leaves. It must've taken him hours.

"No way," I said. "I don't eat cookies made by spies."

I couldn't believe he was even talking to me.

Kids from Siegel House Restaurant and Perfection on a Platter couldn't share lunch. It would be a betrayal.

"Oh . . . ," said Harold. "Okay."

Secretly, I wanted to ask him how he decorated his cookies. I mean, I like to decorate cookies too. But I zipped my lips and made myself say nothing. Harold looked down at his shoes. Then he walked back to his seat.

During art class, Mr. Bloom had us draw pictures of our dream Rosh Hashanah dinner. Harold sat right next to me. I kept bumping his arm. And he kept looking at my paper.

"Are you copying me?" I asked.

He shook his head. "No."

I wrinkled my nose at him. We both made our plates and bowls rainbow colored. He even put crazy straws in his cups, just like me.

"Well," I said, "then why did you draw rainbow plates? That was my idea."

"I like rainbow plates," he said. "They're my favorite kind."

I looked around the art room to see if anyone was looking. There was a question I just had to ask.

"Do you have straws with loop-de-loops at your restaurant?" I asked him.

He grinned at me. His braces reflected the light and were all shiny.

"Big time," he said. "I even have the super-size ones that look like roller coasters."

I've always wanted to buy a pack of the super-size loop-de-loop straws, but Aunt Bean would never let me. She says they're "overly excessive."

I caught myself smiling, and I made myself stop.

When we got back to class, Mrs. Stearns took out six different shofars. Shofars are rams' horns that you blow on Rosh Hashanah. My Uncle Sam blows one at synagogue every year. It makes a super loud sound, and his face always gets red and puffy.

"Let's compare and contrast," said Mrs. Stearns. "What do these shofars have in common?"

That's when I noticed Harold talking quietly to Rachel Rubin.

I leaned in so I could hear what he was saying.

"Here," Harold said, handing Rachel a slip of paper.

Rachel took it.

"Thanks, Harold," she whispered back. She batted her eyelashes at him.

Silently, I nudged Rachel so I could see the slip of paper.

I stared down in horror. It was a coupon. It said: "Rosh Hashanah apple cake at Perfection on a Platter. Buy one, get one free!"

All afternoon, I couldn't look Harold in the eye. Never again would I admire his cookies. There would be no more talking about rainbow dishes or supersize loop-de-loop straws. From here on out, Harold was my enemy. It couldn't be any other way.

Chapter Nine
Whack-a-knee

"Pretty, pretty please," I begged that afternoon. "Please can I use the phone?"

Aunt Lotte sat on the kitchen counter with the phone against her ear. She was talking to her old roommate from college.

"Not right now," she mouthed, waving me away.

I sighed.

This was not going well at all. Rosh Hashanah was only three days away, and things were getting desperate. I really needed to talk to Zadie on the phone.

"Ha-ha," laughed Aunt Lotte into the phone. "That is *heeeeelarious.*"

I crossed my arms. Couldn't Aunt Lotte see that Siegel House was in big, BIG trouble? Couldn't she see that this was the biggest snickerdoodle moment of our lives? Everyone else in the Siegel family was pitching in.

Aunt Bean and Uncle Sam were running the restaurant.

Bubbie was giving everyone noodle necklaces for moral support.

Josh was folding the napkins.

Why did Aunt Lotte waste so much time on the phone? It was almost like she hadn't noticed that Perfection on a Platter was trying to steal our customers.

Typical Aunt Lotte.

I took a deep smell. The air was filled with spice. Sauces swirled away on the stove. They were peppered with pickled radish, shallots, cucumber, and ginger.

Josh dashed down the stairs, his white lab coat streaming behind him.

"Did you call Zadie?" he asked.

I shook my head and pointed to Aunt Lotte. She was talking about the new nail polish color at the local beauty salon. Apparently, you could now paint your nails a color called "Toasty Bagel."

"I have a feeling the phone will be booked all day," I moaned.

Josh opened up his toy doctor's bag and took out a plastic mallet. He whacked me in the knee, and I glared at him.

"What was that for?" I growled.

"It was just to check the knee flex," said Josh.

"You mean knee *re*flex?" I asked.

He nodded. "Yeah . . . knee flex."

I stared at him. I suddenly had a great idea.

"You know, Josh," I said, "Aunt Lotte hasn't been to the doctor in a while. You better check her knee reflexes too!"

He grinned and scampered toward Aunt Lotte. I gave him a thumbs-up as he pulled back the mallet and whacked Aunt Lotte's knee.

"YOOOOOOOOW," she howled.

The phone clattered to the floor.

"Joshua Eliezer Siegel," yelled Aunt Lotte. "What in the world . . . ?"

Before Aunt Lotte could stop me, I grabbed the phone and dialed the hospital's number. Aunt Lotte was so mad, she didn't even notice what I had done.

The phone rang once, twice, a third time . . . "Hospital information desk. How may I help you?" said a lady's voice.

"Hi, I'm Saralee. Is Zadie there?" I asked.

I could hear the lady clicking away on her keyboard.

"I'm sorry, we don't have anyone here by the name of Zadie."

"Well," I explained, "his name is not really Zadie. It's Lev Siegel. He's my grandpa. But I just call him Zadie."

There were more typing sounds.

"He's in room 307. I'll connect you."

I help my breath as the phone rang a second time.

There was a crackly silence.

Then I heard him.

"Yelloo," said Zadie into the phone.

His voice was comforting, like when you dip your finger into a tub of marshmallow fluff. I knew I had only a few moments before Aunt Lotte took the phone back, so I got right to the point.

"Zadie, it's Saralee," I said. "We're in big trouble. The chefs at Perfection on a Platter are horrible and they're . . ."

"Whooo, Saralee. Slow down," interrupted Zadie. "What happened?"

There was too much to explain. The lump in the back of my throat came back. All I wanted was to see and talk to Zadie for real.

"When are you coming home?" I whispered.

"Oh, Saralee, my noggin is all shook up.

And my leg is broken for sure," sighed Zadie. "I've been poked and prodded and poked *again*. And that bump on my head is just getting bigger and redder."

"So what does that mean?" I squeaked. "Can you come home today?"

Zadie cleared his throat.

"Trust me, Saralee," he said. "I've tried sweet-talking my way outta here. Even gave out free louchers for vunch . . ."

"Louchers for vunch?" I asked. "What?"

"I mean free fouchers for funch," said Zadie.

I wrinkled my eyebrows. "Do you mean free vouchers for lunch?"

"Aha!" said Zadie. "Exactly. But the doctors say I gotta stay a little while longer."

My hands grew clammy and cold. I didn't like hearing Zadie get his words mixed up.

"So can you tell me the apple cake secret ingredient?" I said, slowly.

There was silence on the other end of the line.

"Zadie?" I asked. "Are you there?"

"Oh, Saralee," Zadie sighed, "I've been searching my brain high and low. I've looked through all the dusty corners. I've swept away all the cobwebs too."

"And . . . ," I pressed.

"But for the life of me, I cannot remember the secret ingredient," said Zadie. "I'm sorry. But there is *one* thing I do remember."

"What is it?" I asked.

"If you look in the attic, you'll find a . . ."

Zadie trailed off. I could hear voices in the background.

"Gosh, I gotta skedaddle. The doctor's here. Love you, and hugs and kisses to everyone . . ."

"But Zadie, what's in the attic?"

The phone clicked. There was silence on the other end of the line.

"Hey," said Aunt Lotte. She grabbed the phone out of my hands. "I was using that."

I swallowed and looked at Josh. We needed the secret ingredient, and we needed it now. The Perfection on a Platter coupons were going to do serious damage. People in our town LOVE coupons.

"Come on, Josh," I said. "We gotta go to the attic."

Chapter Ten
The Attic

I raced Josh up the stairs to the second-floor landing and pulled down the attic ladder. I took a sniff. The air was different up here. Dusty and musty. The attic was filled with shelves and shelves and more shelves of books. There were boxes stuffed with Passover dishes and old photo albums. A desk sat in the very back of the attic. It was covered with scraps of paper, wrinkled grocery lists, and hundreds of Zadie's old crossword puzzles.

"That's a lot of paper," said Josh. He wasn't kidding. But we needed that ingredient. If Zadie wrote it down, it'd be in here.

"I'll take half the paper, and you take half," I said.

Josh swallowed. "But . . ."

"Come on Josh, you said you wanted to help!"

"I do wanna help," said Josh. "It's just that, Saralee . . ."

"What?"

"I can't read," he said quietly.

"Oh," I said. Sometimes I forget that Josh is only five. "Okay. That's no problem."

I grabbed a crinkled piece of paper from the top of the pile and scavenged for a pen. Then I wrote in big capital letters: APPLE CAKE SECRET INGREDIENT.

"Just look for those words, okay?" I said.

The two of us began. Oh boy, did I wish we had eaten an after-school snack first. Even from up here in the attic, the smell of Siegel House dinner sandwiches wafted up from the kitchen.

Uncle Sam was obviously building works of art from pastrami, sauerkraut, Russian dressing, and slices of thick rye bread. The sandwiches smelled smoky and delicious. They reminded me of an autumn bonfire, where everything is toasty and warm.

It took Josh and me a whole hour to go through all of the papers.

"Did you find anything?" I asked as we neared the bottom of the pile.

Josh looked up. He was sitting on his doctor's bag and holding a piece of paper upside down.

"Nope," he said. "You?"

I shook my head. "No! This is getting really . . ."

But then . . . I smelled the impossible. It was a faint scent. It only lightly dusted my nose receptacles. But it was there all the same.

Josh was staring at me. "Saralee, what are you . . ."

"Shhhhhh," I murmured.

I needed to concentrate. I smelled something sweet yet spicy, zesty yet bland, tart yet un-tart. It was the mystery-ingredient smell! But where was it coming from?

There was no food up here. Josh and I looked everywhere, but there was no mystery food item in sight.

The only interesting thing I found was one of Zadie's old journals. But it was totally useless. It just had slips of ripped paper inside.

I took one of the tiny pieces of paper and read it out loud. It said, *I wish my garden would grow.*

I picked up another one. *I wish my dog wasn't sick.*

Then another one. *I wish to get an A in algebra.* I picked up paper after paper. Each had a wish written on it.

I wish my friend was feeling better.

I wish for health and happiness.

I wish for a puppy. One with spots and a wet nose.

Wishes? Why did Zadie have a journal filled with wishes? Not a single one of those papers had a secret ingredient written on it!

But when I put my nose to the journal's cover, it smelled slightly of apple cake. Maybe this old journal was in the kitchen when Zadie made apple cake last year?

All of a sudden, my stomach growled louder than an industrial-sized dishwasher. It was time for a snack. I carefully carried the journal downstairs to the dining room. Maybe Bubbie, or Aunt Bean, or Uncle Sam could tell me about the journal.

Downstairs, Josh opened the door to the dining room and I looked inside. It was a usual afternoon at Siegel House Restaurant.

"Who's that?" Josh asked, pointing to a table in the corner.

I looked over to where he was pointing and saw a man with a curly mustache and a French beret. He looked very familiar.

"I don't . . ."

In an instant, I realized exactly who I was staring at.

"Oh snickerdoodle," I said under my breath. "I can't believe it."

Chapter Eleven
The Food Critic

There he was, in the flesh. I mean it's one thing to see him on TV. It's another thing to see him *in person* in your own home.

The man was wearing black from head to toe. He was curling his moustache and scribbling in a notepad.

"Follow me," I whispered to Josh.

"Why—"

"*Ssh.* Just follow."

We dashed into the kitchen.

"Saralee," whispered Aunt Bean. "Is that who I think it is?"

Aunt Bean was wearing plastic protectors over her favorite kitty cat shoes. She always did that when she cleaned the floors.

I nodded slowly. "I think so."

Josh smacked his doctor's bag. "What's going on?"

Aunt Bean turned toward Aunt Lotte, who was still gabbing on the phone.

"Put the darn phone down and *help* with this," hissed Aunt Bean.

Aunt Lotte rolled her eyes.

"Help with what?" asked Uncle Sam from across the room. He set down the sandwich he was making and attempted to look into the dining room. But he slipped on the newly cleaned floor, and the platter of sandwiches he was holding went flying. Bread rained down. A glob of mayo landed on Uncle Sam's head.

"Oh snickerdoodle," he mumbled.

There was no time to worry about the ruined sandwiches.

Uncle Sam looked into the dining room again. His face turned white.

"That's . . . that's Mr. Olivetti!" he gasped.

"Oh, Pookie Wookies," sang Bubbie from across the room, "have you seen my dried pasta? I think I've run out!"

No one answered her. There was a world-class food critic sitting in our dining room. The dried pasta would have to wait.

Everyone looked at me. I sniffed a couple of times. *What is everybody looking at?* I thought.

Uncle Sam handed me the menus.

"You should go," he said. "What if he asks a question about food flavors? You're the expert."

I gulped and took the menus. Here's the thing about me and bravery: I'm not a chicken. But I'm also not the fiercest person ever. I have a secret weapon, yes, but having a super-nose is really different from being Superwoman.

Anyway, I walked toward the man and took

two tiny sniffs. He smelled like he'd traveled the world. The scents of exotic spices clung to his clothes. Turmeric. Ajwain seed. Ooh, serrano pepper. He wore many bracelets on his arms; they smelled of the Sahara desert and the Mediterranean Sea.

"Welcome to Siegel House, Mr. Olivetti," I said.

As soon as I said Mr. Olivetti's name, the restaurant grew quiet. People turned around in their seats to catch a glimpse of the famous man.

Boy, was he ever famous. Mr. Olivetti has his own TV show and books. He even has his own salt and pepper shakers with his face on them. He travels around the world trying different foods and writing about them. Everyone knows that a bad review from Mr. Olivetti can destroy a restaurant.

"Can I start you off with something to drink?" I asked him.

"Oh, I'm not ordering anything . . . today," he said, twirling his mustache.

I looked back toward the kitchen. My entire family was peeking at us, trying to hear. I shrugged at them, then turned back to Mr. Olivetti.

He was looking at his fork like he was trying to see his reflection in it.

"You don't want any food?" I stammered.

"No," said Mr. Olivetti. He harrumphed and set the fork back down. "I'm coming back on Friday, right before Rosh Hashanah begins. News has traveled far and wide about your apple cake recipe. However, I hear there's another restaurant in town—and that they're making apple cakes as well."

Here he paused to take a sip of water.

"I love a good competition. When I return, I will try both apple cakes. We'll see which one is best."

He looked right at me.

I felt like taking a step backward, but I held my ground.

Then he said in a low, quiet voice, "May the best restaurant win."

Chapter Twelve
Rumors Gone Wild

A competition?

This was an epic disaster. The most famous, most important food critic in the whole universe was coming back in three days for an apple cake that I couldn't make.

After the food critic left, I went back into the kitchen. Everyone started talking at once.

"What did he want?"

"Why did he leave?"

"Was there a bug?"

"Did you fart?"

"Josh!" My cousin could be so gross. Not that anybody else heard him with all that shouting going on. I put my hands up and shouted even louder, "STOP!"

Everyone froze in their tracks and looked at me.

"He's coming back to taste our apple cake in three days," I said. "And he's trying both our apple cake and Perfection on a Platter's apple cake. It's a competition."

There was silence.

Uncle Sam rubbed his bald head.

"Saralee," he said gravely, "if Mr. Olivetti writes something bad about our restaurant, we're finished."

"I know," I said. This was serious. Now our restaurant's reputation was on the line. If Siegel House went out of business, what would we do? We'd probably have to move away.

Something was burning on the stove. The whole kitchen smelled like a piece of toast had caught on fire and turned into ashes.

"Oh snickerdoodle," Uncle Sam mumbled, running back to the oven.

I looked down at my shoes.

It was up to me. I thought about what Zadie said that night he fell down the stairs:

"I believe in you, Saralee," he had said. We *all* believe in you."

The next day at school, everyone was talking about Mr. Olivetti and the competition.

"Hey Saralee," said Rachel Rubin during pack-up time. "Are your apple cakes ready for the big competition?"

The entire class looked at me. Then they looked at Harold. He was fiddling with his tie, not saying anything.

"Yeah," chimed in Jacob Brodsky. "I heard you couldn't find the secret ingredient . . . is that true?"

I couldn't stand it anymore. I needed to say

something, even if it was a big, fat *lie*. Frantically, I dug through my backpack, looking for something that I could use. My fingers clamped around the journal I'd found in the attic. I pulled it out and waved it in front of the class.

"Actually," I said, in my biggest, loudest voice, "I know the secret ingredient. It's in this journal. So actually we're *not* going to lose."

I shot Harold a look. "So there."

The class stared at the notebook with big round eyes. I wondered if they could tell I was lying.

"Can I touch it?" asked Rachel Rubin.

"Nope," I said, shoving the journal back in my bag. "This is top secret Siegel business. Family only."

Suddenly, there it was *again*. That smell.

The journal smelled slightly sweet yet spicy,

zesty yet bland, tart yet un-tart. None of this made any sense. How could a silly book with ripped-up papers smell like the most delicious apple cake in the world?

I didn't have time to think about it now, though. I had to meet Josh at his kindergarten class so we could walk home. I left my backpack hanging on the cubby hook and dashed back to my desk to grab my scented markers.

It took me a while to find them because they were crammed between my math journal and my vocabulary book. By the time I snatched my backpack and raced over to the kindergarten classroom, Josh was waiting by the door. He was holding a papier-mâché apple he'd made during art class. It was supposed to be a Rosh Hashanah centerpiece, but it looked more like an alien face. Some of the papers were sticking up because he hadn't glued them down.

"Saralee!" Josh called.

He gave me a hug. The handle of his doctor's

bag stuck into my side. I zipped up his jacket and we started for Siegel House.

About halfway home, Josh startled to dawdle.

He held out his smushy papier-mâché apple. "Please?" he asked. "You carry it."

Josh does this literally every time he brings home a project from school.

I sighed and unzipped my backpack.

Huh, I thought. *That's strange.*

I could see the scented markers and my leftover pickles from lunch, but where was the journal?

I riffled through all the different pockets. But the journal was nowhere in sight. I sniffed so hard, my nostrils stuck together for a second. Someone must have stolen the journal while I was getting my smelly markers. I suddenly felt like a piece of wilted lettuce with no dressing.

Everything was falling apart.

This Rosh Hashanah was an absolute disaster.

Chapter Thirteen
Over-Smell

"Are you sad, Saralee?" asked Josh.

The two of us sat on the curb, my backpack still open.

"The journal is gone," I said.

My eyes filled with tears.

"Yeah, but Saralee," said Josh, "the journal didn't have the secret ingredient. It just had a bunch of silly wishes."

I nodded. "I know that. It's just . . . that journal smelled like Zadie's apple cake. Only a little bit, but still. It smelled sweet yet spicy, zesty yet bland, tart yet un-tart . . . It has to be important, it just has to be!"

"Then we have to find it," said Josh.

I scratched my forehead. "But how?"

It was quiet for a second. Then Josh said, "Use your nose. You have the smartest, bestest nose in the whole world."

I looked at him.

I hadn't been feeling great about my secret weapon lately. But maybe Josh was right. Maybe I needed to think less and smell more. I mean, I'm ten now. My nose receptacles are stronger than they've ever been before.

"Okay," I said. "I have an idea. But we'll need my nose and your doctor bag!"

Josh opened his doctor's bag with a *click*.

"Okay," I said. "I need you to wrap an ace bandage around my ears and over my eyes. I don't want to hear or see anything! It's time to go into over-smell."

He quickly did just what I asked.

Soon it was just me and my nose. And the entire world came alive.

The wind smelled of pumpkin, and fresh apples, and popcorn slathered with melted butter and cinnamon. I could smell the Siegel House pickles from over three streets away. Even from here I could pick out the kosher dill, the bread and butter pickles, the jalapeño pickles, and the half-sours.

I could smell everything from every street in town.

Now all I needed to do was focus.

In all the smells, I needed to find just one—a smell that was sweet yet spicy, zesty yet bland, tart yet un-tart. I sniffed through the extra smells, setting them aside, pushing them away. And finally, I found the one scent I was looking for.

"Gotcha!" I yelled.

Josh held my hand as we raced down the busy sidewalks. I sniffed and smelled and breathed in and out. I tracked that smell until we reached the source.

I let go of Josh's clammy hand and lifted the bandage from my eyes.

We stood in front of a shop. I cringed as I saw four words painted on the door.

Perfection on a Platter.

Chapter Fourteen
Perfection on a Platter

The door to Perfection on a Platter swung open. A few customers walked down the steps and onto the sidewalk.

Josh and I darted behind a nearby bush.

I sniffed inward.

Yep, the journal was most certainly in there. That meant only one thing: Harold "the horror" Horowitz had stolen it out of my backpack. My nostrils flared up in rage.

"Come on," I whispered to Josh. "Let's go

through the side entrance."

We darted to the side of the building and scampered inside. Before anyone noticed, we ducked behind the nearest table.

Perfection on a Platter was like nothing I had seen before.

The walls were painted neon colors. Instead of Bubbie leading everyone to their seats (and sometimes getting lost), there was a seating hostess robot.

Josh opened his doctor's bag and took out his magnifying glass.

"Whoa," he said, pointing to the hostess robot.

It was tall and made of metal. It said things like "This way, please" and "Follow me, sir."

I seriously couldn't believe what I was seeing. In the middle of the dining room was the largest platter I had ever seen. It was filled with chopped veggies, fruits, and different types of crackers. There were lots of dips too. My nose could detect three-bean dip, hummus, and some strange olive oil concoction. All of the customers were plunging their veggies into the dips.

Some were double-dipping.

"Ew, gross," I muttered. "They should call this place 'Germs on a Platter.'"

Josh laughed.

"All right," I said. "You look under the rest of the tables. I'll search the kitchen."

But before we could move, five suited figures walked out of the kitchen. I gulped. It was the Horowitz family. And with them was Harold. He held the journal in his hands. My stomach twisted in anger when I saw him. All this time, he had pretended to be so nice. All that stuff about rainbow plates and supersize roller-coaster twisty straws was just an act.

"What are they doing?" asked Josh.

"Shh," I whispered. "I'm trying to hear."

The Horowitz family gathered around a table in a corner of the restaurant. Harold taped a sign to the back of his chair. It said: Family Meeting. Do Not Disturb.

"I have to get over there," I said. "Josh, you stay here. Whatever you do, don't move."

Chapter Fifteen
Doctor Josh

I scampered toward the platter in the middle of the room. From behind the cracker display, I could hear the Horowitzes arguing.

The suited lady slammed the journal on the table.

"This book is filled with wishes," she hissed. "It's useless! Harold—you were supposed to get the secret ingredient."

Soon everyone was snarling at each other.

"How are we going to win the competition now?" said a suited man.

"Yeah," chimed in another Horowitz. "You promised we would win."

The terrible family was so embroiled in their argument that the suited lady accidentally knocked the journal off the table. It lay on the floor now.

This was my chance. The journal was brimming with the scent of apple cake. I inched my way toward it. Yes, I was in enemy territory. But that apple cake smell pulled me forward. My nostrils hummed. My nose receptacles tingled and buzzed.

I tiptoed my way toward the table and wrapped my hands around that journal.

But someone else did too.

I looked up.

It was Harold Horowitz. His eyes were wide. His face was pale.

"Saralee?" he whispered. "What're you doing here?"

I pulled on the journal. Harold pulled back. We were in a deadlock. Harold was just too strong, and my fingers were growing weak. As I pulled, the journal smelled more and more like apple cake.

I pulled harder, but Harold was taller than me. His arms looked way stronger too. I closed my eyes and tugged with all my might. I wished with all my heart that Zadie would come home for Rosh Hashanah. If he hadn't broken his leg and bumped his head, then none of this would have happened.

The apple cake smell grew even stronger.

I wish for Zadie, I thought. *I wish for Zadie, I WISH FOR ZADIE.*

I sniffed. All I could smell was apple cake. Delicious, golden-brown apple cake.

Without warning, Josh let out a yell.

"KNEE FLEX!" he shouted.

All the suits turned around. Josh ran forward and whacked Harold in the knee with his plastic mallet.

The journal went flying. The pages flew open and all the wishes fluttered to the floor. Suddenly, the apple cake smell was so powerful, my nose felt like it would explode.

The wishes smelled sweet yet spicy, zesty yet bland, tart yet un-tart.

Wishes . . .

Why did the wishes smell like apple cake?

Could it really be so simple?

Zadie's voice filled my head. I remembered the song he always sang before Rosh Hashanah.

A sweet new year.

A sweet new year.

Make a wish for a sweet new year.

"That's it!" I yelled, grabbing the journal and a handful of wishes off the floor. I knew what the secret ingredient was. My nose had known it all along. How could I have missed Zadie's clue?

"Run, Josh," I shouted.

The two of us streaked out the door. I smiled as I ran. I knew the secret ingredient now. Rosh Hashanah was saved.

"Hey! Come back, you bratty kids!" called the suited lady. But we didn't stop running. I smelled apple cake the whole way home.

Chapter Sixteen
Never Say Never

A few minutes later, Josh and I burst into the Siegel House kitchen.

"I know the secret ingredient!" I shouted.

The whole family looked up. I thrust the journal in the air.

"Zadie was collecting wishes," I explained. "Wishes are the secret ingredient!"

Aunt Lotte hung up the phone.

Uncle Sam squeezed the ketchup bottle so hard, he got red stuff all over his apron.

Even Aunt Bean dropped the dustpan.

"But how?" she asked. "That's impossible. A wish can't be a secret ingredient. This will never work."

I looked at Bubbie. She winked at me.

"Never say never," I said, smiling. "You never know. A little wish goes a long way."

"All right," said Uncle Sam. "Let's try it."

Everyone wrote down a random wish on a piece of paper. Then I drew one from the pile. It was Aunt Lotte's.

I gathered the rest of the ingredients and began my apple cake. I added the flour, sugar, honey, and apples. The whole family clustered around me as I mixed the cake batter.

"All right, Aunt Lotte," I said. "Close your eyes and make your wish."

Aunt Lotte touched the batter bowl and started muttering about a bright red convertible with flames on the side.

I jiggled the bowl.

I counted to three.

I even waved my fingers over it.

But nothing smelled sweet yet spicy, zesty yet bland, tart yet un-tart.

"Ummm," said Aunt Lotte, "is something supposed to happen?

Suddenly, my heart felt heavy like a matzah ball sinking to the bottom of a bowl.

"It didn't work," I whispered. "I really thought I had figured it out."

Bubbie started to hum a tune.

A sweet new year.
A sweet new year.
Make a wish for a sweet new year.

I looked up.

"Wait a minute!" I shouted. "That song isn't about any old wishes. It's about *New Year's* wishes."

"You mean . . . ," Uncle Sam started.

I nodded.

"A New Year's wish!" I said excitedly. "Rosh

Hashanah is the start of the new year. So the secret ingredient is a *New Year's* wish!"

I held the batter bowl between my hands. This was the most important moment of my life. If this worked . . . Siegel House would be saved.

I whispered my Rosh Hashanah wish under my breath. Then I closed my eyes and stood perfectly still. I thought about the wish so hard, I could hear it rattling around in my brain.

All of a sudden, my nostrils began to tingle.

The smell was weak at first. It only lightly brushed my nose receptacles. But then it grew stronger and stronger until . . .

"Oh my stars," said Bubbie.

I took a giant sniff. It was the apple cake smell! It filled every nook and cranny of the kitchen, growing more powerful by the second.

"It's sweet yet spicy," boomed Uncle Sam.

"Zesty yet bland," yelled Aunt Lotte.

"Tart yet un-tart," squeaked Aunt Bean. "I can't believe it."

I opened my eyes and grinned from ear to ear. I had finally made Zadie's Rosh Hashanah apple cake. It was so simple. All I needed to do was whisper a New Year's wish while making the batter. It didn't matter if the wish was big or small or somewhere in-between. It didn't matter who made the wish or why they had made the wish. There just needed to be one New Year's wish in every apple cake.

I looked at the large pile of order forms and gulped.

I'd need a ton of wishes by tomorrow.

Chapter Seventeen
Wish Collector

The next day, I collected Rosh Hashanah wishes from everyone at school. I even went to the principal's office during recess (on purpose).

"Saralee!" Mr. Rosen called, as I walked into his office. "How can I help you on this fine day?"

"I'm here to ask you a question," I said.

He opened his office door, and I went inside. The walls were painted completely brown. He even had brown paintings hanging in brown picture frames.

"Yes?" Mr. Rosen asked. "Please don't tell me that the apple cakes are being canceled. I heard a terrible rumor that . . ."

I swatted the air. "Oh, don't worry about that. No, I just wanted to ask—this Rosh Hashanah, what's your New Year's wish?"

Mr. Rosen tilted his head to the side.

"You know," he said, "your zadie always asks me that question every year before Rosh Hashanah. And every year I tell him the same thing. I wish for apple cake!"

By that afternoon, I had collected a whole bag of wishes.

Then I saw Harold.

Harold the Horror.

He was the only person at school I hadn't asked.

He was sitting on the fuzzy carpet, flipping through a colorful cookbook. I was still mad at him. But I guessed it wouldn't hurt to ask about his wish.

"Hi, Harold," I said.

"Hi."

His cheeks turned pink. He was probably embarrassed that he stole my zadie's journal from my backpack.

"Can I ask you a question?" I asked.

"Sure."

"Do you have a New Year's wish for this Rosh Hashanah?"

He gave me a funny look.

"I thought it would be obvious," he said.

I narrowed my eyes. "What do you mean?"

Harold sighed. "I wish you'd be my friend, Saralee."

I stared at him. This was unbelievable!

"Why would you want to be my friend?" I asked. "We are enemies. Don't you know that?"

Harold shrugged.

"I don't know," he said. "You like to cook,

just like me. And you like twisty straws. And you like rainbow dishes. No one at my old school liked that stuff."

"Yeah, well, friends don't steal other friends' journals," I said.

His face turned even redder. It matched the color of his hair.

"I didn't want to steal it," he said.

"Then why did you do it?"

He fiddled with his tie. "If your family needed you . . . wouldn't you help them? I know they're not perfect . . . but family is family."

I didn't know what to say, so I wrote down his wish and put it in the bag.

"What do you think?" he asked. "Will you . . . you know . . ."

I scratched my nose.

"Can I think about it?" I asked.

He nodded.

Then he gave me a cookie. This time I ate it. I hate to say it, but it was actually pretty good.

Chapter Eighteen
The Taste Battle

That day, after school, my family started on the baking. Never in my life have we worked so hard. Around me, I could smell sugar and apples—and, of course, that indescribable scent of a Rosh Hashanah wish.

It was my job to whisper the wishes over the apple cake batter. There were so many, each one different.

I wish to do my homework on time.
I wish to be nicer to my mom.

I wish to see a rainbow this year.

I wish for love.

I looked around the kitchen. It was filled with apple cakes. Perfectly golden-brown, absolutely scrumptious apple cakes.

Though everything was beautiful, I still felt a little sad inside.

Zadie wasn't here to see this.

I walked over to the phone and dialed Zadie's room in the hospital. It rang and rang, but Zadie didn't pick up.

When I heard the message beep, I swallowed hard.

"Hi Zadie," I squeaked. "This is Saralee. I just wanted to tell you that I love you, and I found the secret ingredient. I miss you, Zadie. Come home."

The next day was erev Rosh Hashanah, which meant that the holiday would start at sundown. It was also the day of the competition.

We closed the restaurant after breakfast, and I made the apple cake for Mr. Olivetti. Then we headed to the town square for the apple cake taste-off. I gulped when I saw the crowd. Everyone I knew was there: all my friends from fifth grade, all of our usual customers, even the mailman.

In the middle of the crowd was a beautifully set table.

My family stood on one side.

The Horowitzes stood on the other.

Harold was in front. He held an apple cake. He smiled at me. I gave him a teensy, tiny, almost barely visible smile back.

Of course, I wanted to win this competition. But I sorta hoped that Mr. Olivetti would like Harold's apple cake too. Just as long as he liked mine better.

I mean, Harold wasn't all bad. And maybe we could cook together sometime? Harold's the only other kid in my class who can make sugar cookies from scratch.

Anyway, it was precisely noon when Mr. Olivetti arrived.

A hush fell over the crowd.

Mr. Olivetti strolled toward the table, sat down, and draped the napkin over his lap.

"It's time," whispered Uncle Sam. "Go do your thing, Saralee."

Taking a deep breath, I walked toward Mr. Olivetti, clutching my apple cake firmly in my hands. I hoped Zadie would be proud of me. I hoped the apple cake was tasty enough.

Harold and I placed our apple cakes before Mr. Olivetti. We all watched as he picked up his fork.

Mr. Olivetti tried the Perfection on a Platter apple cake first. He scratched his chin, then took a sip of water.

"Very good," he said.

Then he pointed to our apple cake.

"So, this is the famous Siegel apple cake," he said.

I nodded. The crowd was so silent, I could hear Aunt Lotte chewing her bubble gum.

"Yes," I said. "This is it."

Mr. Olivetti carefully cut himself a slice and took a bite. No one moved. No one breathed. Everyone just watched Mr. Olivetti chew.

At first, he didn't say a word.

I know this because I watched his lips as I strained my ears to hear him.

Then, slowly, his lips spread into a huge smile.

"In all my life," he said, "I've never tasted anything so wonderful!"

Inside me, I felt this indescribable feeling. It was like butter and cinnamon melting inside my heart.

"If you don't mind me asking," he said, "what did you put in this cake? I've never tasted anything like it. It . . . it tastes sweet yet spicy, zesty yet bland, tart yet un-tart. It seems impossible."

I looked at my family. They were grinning from ear to ear.

"It's a secret, Mr. Olivetti," I said. "But let's just say, everyone *wishes* they knew our secret ingredient."

Uncle Sam winked at me.

Then, as Mr. Olivetti twirled his moustache in thought, the whole town lined up for their Rosh Hashanah orders.

Funny enough, a lot of people bought two apple cakes. One from Siegel House and one from Perfection on a Platter.

Jacob Brodsky held both of his boxes in the air. "Hey, Harold. Hey, Saralee. I'm going to gobble these up tonight," he shouted.

Harold and I looked at each other.

I guess Zadie was right. People really do have large appetites around here.

"Can I try a slice of your apple cake?" asked Harold. "It sounds delicious."

I looked at my family. They were busy handing out the apple cake boxes.

"All right," I said. "And maybe . . . I'll try a bite of yours too."

Chapter Nineteen
The Final Wish

Here's something about my family: we eat a lot—especially on holidays. That night, the restaurant was closed for the holiday. All of us Siegels bustled around with our own last-minute Rosh Hashanah dinner preparations.

"We have enough food to feed an army," fretted Aunt Bean.

Aunt Lotte set the table with fancy dishes. Josh took out a plastic thermometer. He opened the oven door to take the temperature of the turkey.

"No!" shouted Uncle Sam. "That's plastic, it's gonna melt."

SMASH!

An entire bowl of apple slices fell off the counter.

"Whoopsie-daisy," he sighed. "I better get more apples from the grocery. We're out."

Then he pointed at Josh. "Stay away from that oven, okay? Let's not burn the house down."

Poor Uncle Sam practically ran out the door.

Even though the table looked beautiful, my insides felt like soggy cereal. Zadie still wasn't here. It was the first Rosh Hashanah I had ever spent without him.

All I wanted to do was give Zadie a great big bear hug. I wanted to tell him about how I'd collected wishes and about Mr. Olivetti. I tried the hospital again, but no one picked up the phone.

"When's Zadie coming home?" I asked Aunt Bean.

She patted my back.

"Oh, Saralee," she said. "I have no idea. Let's hope it's sooner rather than later."

Soon Uncle Sam came back and dinner was

ready. In the kitchen, the last apple cake sat quietly on the counter. It was golden brown, and it looked wonderful. I reached out and touched the side of the apple cake.

I closed my eyes and made a wish. It was the same secret wish I'd made before.

I wish Zadie was here, I thought. I wished so hard, all I could hear was the wish bouncing around inside my head.

Suddenly, there was a knock on the door. I opened one eye, then the other. *Could it be?*

"Saralee, go open it," called Uncle Sam.

Slowly, I walked to the door. My nose was filled with the smells of Rosh Hashanah. I could smell the roasted turkey and potatoes. I could smell the apples and the honey. But more than anything, I could smell all those New Year's wishes.

And then I smelled something else. I smelled peppermint and just the slightest bit of corned beef on rye. I knew that smell from somewhere . . .

"Zadie!" I shouted.

I threw the door open wide.

"SURPRISE!" yelled Zadie.

There he was, smiling at me. His leg was in a cast and his arms were resting on crutches. My dear, sweet Zadie.

I threw my arms around him, careful not to knock his crutches free. He smelled just the same.

"You're back!" I cried, holding him close.

As we stood in the doorway, the whole family gathered around us.

"Surprise, Saralee!" they shouted.

Bubbie just beamed. Uncle Sam hadn't really gone to the grocery store. He had picked up Zadie from the hospital. How sneaky!

"Is dinner ready yet?" asked Zadie. "I'm starving!"

Everyone laughed.

I pulled Zadie into the kitchen and set a slice of apple cake in front of him. I didn't think anyone would mind if a little nibble was missing.

Zadie sniffed it. He rotated the plate, then sniffed it again. Then he crossed his arms and narrowed his eyes at me. I crossed my arms and narrowed my eyes back at him.

"You figured it out," he said. "Even with my brain all muddled up, you figured it out."

Then he laughed and laughed, and I laughed with him. "How did you do it, Saralee?" he asked. "How did you figure out Zadie's secret ingredient?"

"I have a secret weapon, remember?" I said. "My nose can smell anything . . . even a New Year's wish."

Zadie's eyes got all sparkly. He put his arm around my shoulder.

"My Saralee," he said. "With a nose like that, you'll surely rule the world."

The End